Published in 2023
by Vision Australia
454 Glenferrie Road,
Kooyong, Victoria 3144

Produced by
Berbay Publishing
PO Box 133
Kew East
Victoria 3102

Vision Australia gratefully acknowledges
the generous support from The Elliot Family Trust.

Printed in China

National Library of Australia
Cataloguing-in-publication data:
Dickson, John
Matt Formston: Surfing in the Dark

For primary school children
ISBN 978-0-6455584-0-1

MATT FORMSTON

SURFING IN THE DARK

Written by John Dickson
Illustrated by Philip Bunting

Matt Formston is a world champion surfer.
When Matt listens, the ocean tells him things.
When he touches the ocean, he feels its secrets.
But when he looks at the ocean, he cannot see it.
Matt is almost completely blind.

Braille

Matt hid his blindness so well when he was little that nobody knew he was finding it harder and harder to see. He could run, he could chase, he could kick a ball, climb a tree and ride a bike better than all the other kids.

But by the time he was five years old, all he could see was a big black dot in the middle of his eyes, with some blurry shapes around the outside of it.

Matt's mum and dad decided that his life would be as normal as they could possibly make it.

He would continue to play sport. He would go to school with all the other kids. The word 'can't' would never be used.

When Matt went to school, he sat in the front row of the class. Teachers thought this might help him see the chalkboard. But Matt couldn't see the chalkboard. The words in Matt's books were made bigger. But they were no easier to read. Matt came up with a plan. He asked his teachers questions. Lots of questions. All the time.

Some people are scared to ask questions. Not Matt. Asking questions has helped Matt all his life.

Matt is not frightened of making mistakes, either. He quickly discovered that in each mistake there was something to learn.

When he was growing up, Matt's neighbourhood included professional surfers, rock stars and famous footballers. Matt wanted to be like them. He never wanted to be just 'the blind kid'. He wanted to be a professional surfer.

In the surf, Matt's dad or his big brother would plonk him on a boogie board and throw him in front of a wave.

Matt would shoot towards the shore, where his dad would be waiting to take him back to the waves for another ride. Over and over again.

Matt began to hear what the water had to tell him. 'If you lie too far forward, your board will sink and throw you off. If you lie too far back, your board will slip off the wave and you will stop.'

Second to riding his boogie board, Matt loved playing rugby. He would often go with his dad to his big brother's games. Matt would sit with the adults, who would describe the game to him. Matt listened carefully and asked many questions.

Matt knew that knowledge would give him an advantage. He also knew that he had to be strong and fit.

Every day before school, Matt would ride his bike and run for kilometres. Nobody in the rugby team was as fit as Matt Formston. When Matt decided to do something, he planned to be the very best. He didn't just want to be a player, he wanted to be good enough to be the team captain.

One day in the surf, a girl refused to speak to Matt because she was on a surfboard and he was only on a boogie board. She called it 'an esky lid'. That was the day Matt started riding surfboards. He was eleven years old.

The ocean had already told him many things. But there was more to learn standing on a surfboard.

Day after day, Matt would hit the surf and the surf would hit him. Again, he was making mistakes. Again, he was learning. Every time he surfed, he got better at it. Nothing would make him stop.

Then he got sick.

Matt was 16 years old when he got glandular fever. It made him feel tired and he had no energy. It took him nearly a year to recover. By the time he was ready to play rugby again, it was too late. All the skills he had developed had faded. While he was sick, his teammates had become bigger and stronger, faster and smarter. Matt no longer fitted in.

NARRABEEN
NSW

He became angry with the world. He left home to live alone. But even though he could no longer do the things he loved, Matt continued to ask questions and learn from his mistakes.

And he continued training to be super fit. He never stopped.

Eventually, he was offered a job with a company that would help him be his very best.

When he decided to do a 1200-kilometre bike ride for charity, his life changed again. Matt was asked to become a cycling Paralympian.

He wanted to be a world champion and a world record holder in three years. His coach laughed and said that it couldn't be done.

Matt did it in four.

With his cycling pilot on the front of their tandem, he went on to win titles and break records all over the world.

But soon, all he could hear was the ocean calling. It was time to return to his dream: to become the pro surfer he had envied all those years ago.

Matt wanted to tackle the waves that even surfers who can see would think twice about riding.

His coach knew better than to get in his way. Riding a jet ski, the coach would tow Matt into the path of a wave, tell him when to 'go' and leave him to it. Wave after wave after wave.

Now Matt is a world champion. Again. And he's planning to win gold for Australia at the 2028 Paralympic Games.

Matt says, 'People ask me, if I could go back to being five years old and choose to be sighted, would I do it? My eyesight has driven me to take all the opportunities that have come my way. I would keep my disability because it made me who I am.'

GLOSSARY

Cycling pilot

An able-bodied cyclist who rides with a vision-impaired cyclist. The pilot sits at the front and steers the bicycle.

Glandular fever

Glandular fever is an illness caused by a virus, which is a type of germ you can catch from other people. If you catch glandular fever, you might have high fevers, lumps around your throat and you might feel very tired.

Paralympic Games

A sporting competition for disabled athletes, held after the Olympic Games. A person who competes in the Paralympic Games is called a Paralympian.